HALLOWEEN TREATS

Books by Carolyn Haywood

Summer Fun 1986
Merry Christmas from Eddie 1986
How the Reindeer Saved Santa 1986
Happy Birthday from Carolyn Haywood 1984
Santa Claus Forever! 1983
Halloween Treats 1981
The King's Monster 1980
Eddie's Menagerie 1978
Betsy's Play School 1977
A Valentine Fantasy 1976
Eddie's Valuable Property 1975
"C" Is for Cupcake 1974
Away Went the Balloons 1973
A Christmas Fantasy 1972
Eddie's Happenings 1971
Merry Christmas from Betsy 1970
Taffy and Melissa Molasses 1969
Ever-Ready Eddie 1968
Betsy and Mr. Kilpatrick 1967
Eddie the Dog Holder 1966
Robert Rows the River 1965
Eddie's Green Thumb 1964
Here Comes the Bus! 1963
Snowbound with Betsy 1962

Annie Pat and Eddie 1960
Eddie and Louella 1959
Betsy's Winterhouse 1958
Eddie Makes Music 1957
Betsy's Busy Summer 1956
Eddie and His Big Deals 1955
Betsy and the Circus 1954
Eddie's Pay Dirt 1953
The Mixed-Up Twins 1952
Eddie and Gardenia 1951
Betsy's Little Star 1950
Eddie and the Fire Engine 1949
Penny Goes to Camp 1948
Little Eddie 1947
Penny and Peter 1946
Betsy and the Boys 1945
Here's a Penny 1944
Back to School with Betsy 1943
Primrose Day 1942
Betsy and Billy 1941
Two and Two Are Four 1940
"B" Is for Betsy 1939

CAROLYN HAYWOOD

HALLOWEEN TREATS

ILLUSTRATED BY VICTORIA DE LARREA

Troll Associates

A TROLL BOOK, published by Troll Associates,
Mahwah, NJ 07430

Published by arrangement with William Morrow and Company, Inc. For information address William Morrow and Company, Inc., 105 Madison Avenue, New York, New York 10016.

First Troll Printing, 1987

Printed in the United States of America

10 9 8 7 6 5 4 3 2 1

ISBN 0-8167-1039-2

Dedicated with love to
Thelma Hart,
Imogene, April,
and
Earl Hart.

CONTENTS

Chapter 1

THE WITCH AND THE BALLOON

KATIE AND MARK were twins. Early in October they moved into a house on a narrow street where all the houses stood cheek to cheek in a line. The back of each house looked out upon a small yard with a high wooden fence.

The children soon learned, from other children on the block, that a woman lived by herself in the house next door to them. They were told that her name was Mrs. Biggs and that no one ever saw her. Once a week a car stopped at the door, and a man carried a large bag into Mrs. Biggs's house. The man never stayed more than a few minutes, and no one knew who he was.

Although Mrs. Biggs kept herself hidden, Katie and Mark heard her whenever they made any noise. Then she knocked loudly on the wall between the two houses. Each time the children became more and more curious about this neighbor who was sometimes heard but never seen.

One day, when the children were playing in the bedroom at the back of the house, Katie kicked the table and upset a game of checkers that Mark was just about to win. Mark yelled, "Clumsy! Look what you did!"

Katie yelled back at Mark, "Well, it's your fault! You kicked me under the table."

Then Mark kicked the table too and upset it completely. Above the noise came a knocking on the wall. The children looked at each other, and they both said in a whisper, "That's Biggy!" For the rest of the afternoon they were quiet.

Once Mrs. Biggs knocked so hard that a picture on the wall fell down.

"What do you think she uses to knock with?" Mark asked Katie.

"Her stick, of course!" Katie replied. "I'm sure she walks around with a big, thick stick. I think she's a witch. That's what I think."

That same day the children heard the bang of a heavy lid. The sound came from Mrs. Biggs's yard. Katie jumped up. "Oh, quick, Markie!" she called out, as she ran to the window. "I think Biggy's putting out her garbage. Now we'll see her."

Mark joined Katie at the window just as the lid banged again. The children looked down, but all they saw was a black cat sitting on top of a short roof that extended out over Mrs. Biggs's kitchen. "We'll never see that old woman!" said Mark.

"Do you see that black cat, Mark?" asked Katie. "That's her cat. Witches always have black cats."

The following Saturday morning Katie looked out her bedroom window down into the yard next door. She could hardly believe what she saw, for there, caught on Mrs. Biggs's clothesline was a balloon. "Mark! Mark!" Katie called out. "Come here, Mark."

Mark came from his room in his pajamas, rubbing his eyes. "Why did you wake me up?" he asked. "Don't you know it's Saturday?"

"Of course, I know it's Saturday," Katie replied. "But just see what's on Biggy's clothesline."

Mark stared down. "Creepers!" he said. "It's an orange balloon, and it's painted to look like a jack-o'-lantern."

"She couldn't have washed a balloon and put it out to dry," said Katie.

"Of course not!" said Mark. "The wind blew the balloon into the yard, and it's caught on the line. I wish I could get it. I wish the wind had blown it into our yard."

"I don't see how you can get it," said Katie.

"I could put the stepladder against the fence and climb over," said Mark.

"How would you get back without the stepladder on the other side?" Katie asked.

"Well, maybe if I just rang the front doorbell and asked for the balloon, she'd give it to me," said Mark.

Katie looked at Mark with horror. "Oh, you wouldn't," she said. "She's a witch! She'd grab you and pull you in. Probably she'd fatten you up and cook you like that witch in *Hansel and Gretel.*"

Then Katie pointed to the clothesline again. "Do you see that fuzzy thing hanging on the line?" she asked.

"You mean right under the balloon?" Mark asked.

"That's right," said Katie, nodding her head. "Do you know what it is?"

"No!" replied Mark. "What is it?"

"It's the skin of a cat," said Katie. "You know that black cat that we saw sitting on her kitchen roof one day?"

"Uh-huh!" said Mark, looking at Katie with wide eyes.

"Well, that's its skin," said Katie. "Old Biggy took the cat and skinned it and cooked it."

"Cooked the cat?" Mark exclaimed.

"Sure!" Katie replied. "She's a witch! Witches always cook cats. It's the way they make their brew."

Mark whistled. "She's a baddy all right!" he exclaimed.

By the end of the day, when the children looked down into Mrs. Biggs's yard, the balloon and the cat skin were no longer there.

"Now look!" said Katie. "She's taken the balloon inside her house."

"Oh, I hope she hasn't given it away," said Mark.

"Who would she give it to?" said Katie. "Nobody goes into her house but that man with the bag. He wouldn't want a Halloween balloon!"

"You don't know," said Mark. "Maybe he has kids. Oh, why did it have to blow into her yard. Why didn't it blow into ours?"

As Halloween drew nearer, Katie and Mark thought more and more about their next-door neighbor. "I know she's a witch," said Katie. "I'm sure she'll ride on her broomstick on Halloween. I'm going to watch at the window all evening, and I'll bet I'll see her go off on her broomstick."

"Aren't you going out trick or treating?" Mark asked.

"Oh, no!" said Katie. "I wouldn't want to miss seeing her ride off on her broomstick. You can go trick or treating by yourself."

"Well," said Mark, "I guess it would be more fun to see her ride on her broomstick, especially if we're the only kids to see her. Do you think she'll go out the front door or the back door, Katie?"

"Oh, she'll go out a window," said Katie. "I'm sure she'll go out a window. She'll get up speed quicker that way."

"That's right," said Mark.

When Halloween arrived, Katie and Mark had no interest in dressing up as they had in other years. They just wanted to watch for a witch on a broomstick, and they were certain that she would come out of the house next door.

The children waited until dusk, and then each went to a window. "After all," said Katie, "she won't go off until it gets dark. Witches never do."

Katie took her place at the back window and Mark at the front window. "Remember, we're going to call each other if we see anything," said Katie.

After a long time, Katie got tired of standing, so she drew up a chair and sat down.

Mark sat on the arm of the big stuffed chair with his nose glued to the windowpane.

After a while, Katie heard a window being raised in Mrs. Biggs's house. "Markie!" Katie called to her brother. "Come quick. I think she's about to take off. I heard her raise the window."

Mark came running to Katie. They both were so excited that they could feel their hearts pounding.

With their eyes bulging, they waited and waited, but they saw nothing emerge from the window next door. The night grew later and later. Finally Mark said, "I don't think she is going to come out of that window. I'm going back to the front window."

Mark left Katie, who now had her arms on the windowsill and her head on her arms, and returned to his seat on the arm of the chair. In a while he slid into the chair. Soon he was sound asleep. Not long after Katie was asleep too.

When their parents came upstairs to go to bed, they found the children sound asleep. So their mother took Katie and their father took Mark and led them to their rooms. Then their parents helped them to undress and tucked them into bed.

The children had fallen into a deep sleep, when suddenly Mark was wakened by a sound. He listened. There it was again. Someone was knocking, knocking on the wall beside his bed. Mark thought of Mrs. Biggs. It must be Mrs. Biggs who was knocking. Then Mark heard a church clock strike two. Again there was the knock beside his bed. Why would Mrs. Biggs be knocking when he wasn't making any noise at all!

Mark slid out of bed. He went out into the dark hall and ran to his parents' room. "Daddy, Daddy!" he called, as he opened their door.

His father woke up. "What's the matter?" he asked.

"Biggy's knocking," said Mark. "She's knocking on my wall."

Mark's father got up and followed Mark to his room. They both listened. *Knock, knock, knock.*

Soon Katie was awake. She came to the door. "What's the matter?" she asked.

"Biggy's knocking," Mark replied.

"Why, were you making a lot of noise?" Katie asked.

"'Course not!" said Mark. "How could I make a lot of noise when I was asleep?"

Knock, knock, knock came again from the other side of the wall.

"I'm afraid something has happened to the old lady," said their father. "Maybe she fell and can't get up. I think she's calling for help."

"You mean she wants you to go in her house?" Katie said in an awed voice. "Don't forget. She's a witch. She might turn you into a frog or something even worse."

Katie's father didn't pay any attention to her. Instead he said, "I'll have to call the police. I have no way of getting to her."

At this point Katie and Mark were wide awake, and so was their mother. The whole family was pattering around in bathrobes and slippers.

"Maybe we better knock on the wall so that she'll know we've heard her," said their mother.

"I'll knock," said Mark. "I'll knock with Daddy's shoe."

Mark felt strange to be knocking on Mrs. Biggs's wall. It was like speaking to someone whom he never had seen.

By the time the police car arrived, the children's father was dressed. The police asked a lot of questions. "Do you have a key? Do you know someone to call? Do you know the name of the man who comes every week?"

The answer to all the questions was "No."

"We'll have to see if there is an open window," said one policeman. With the help of a ladder, the policemen and the children's father climbed over the wooden fence into Mrs. Biggs's yard. They looked at all the windows. A little window in the bathroom was open.

"Somebody will have to get in through that window," said one of the policemen.

"It isn't possible," said the other policeman. "Only a child could get in there."

Mark was dressed and looking over the top of the fence from the ladder. His father looked at him and said, "Markie, I guess it's up to you!"

Katie was standing at the open window in the upstairs bedroom. When she heard her father speak to Mark, she shouted down, "No, no, Markie! Don't go in there. She's a witch!"

"Oh, rats!" said Mark, as he dropped over the fence into a policeman's arms.

Soon the three men had a ladder placed beneath the bathroom window. "Now, Mark," said one of the policemen, "you start up the ladder. I'll be right behind you, and I'll push you through the window. When you get inside, call to the old lady and say, 'Everything is all right! We've come to help you.' "

"Okay!" said Mark, as he started up the ladder. When he reached the window, there was just room enough for Mark to wriggle through. He dropped from the windowsill to the floor.

The policeman, holding a flashlight, spoke to Mark from outside. "Switch on the lights," he said.

Mark turned on the light and called out. "I'm coming, Mrs. Biggs! We're coming to help you."

Mark found the light switch in the hall, and then he made his way easily to the room where he knew Mrs. Biggs must be. The light from the hall was strong enough to show him a tiny old lady lying on the floor.

"Oh, it's good of you to come to me," said Mrs. Biggs. "I fell over the cat, and I can't get up. Mandy's so black that I can't see her in the dark."

"Soon as I run down and open the kitchen door, my father and two policemen will come up," said Mark, already in the hall.

"Oh, come back! Come back!" said Mrs. Biggs.

"I don't want them to see me without my wig. It's right there on the dresser. All clean, it is. I washed it last week and hung it out to dry."

"Is this it?" said Mark, holding up what Katie had said was the skin of the black cat.

"That's it," said Mrs. Biggs.

While Mrs. Biggs was adjusting her wig Mark ran down to the back door and let the three men into the house. "What took you so long?" his father asked.

"She had to put on her wig," said Mark.

The men laughed as they came into the kitchen. Mark's father went upstairs while the policemen brought a stretcher.

The policemen were very kind and gentle, and before long they had Mrs. Biggs on the stretcher. As they were about to lift her, she stretched out her hand to Mark. "It was good of you to come," she said again. "I'd like to give you something, but I don't know what."

"What about the balloon?" said Mark. "Katie and I would like to have the jack-o'-lantern balloon."

"Of course, you can have the balloon. Funny how it just blew into the yard and got stuck on my clothesline," said Mrs. Biggs.

"Oh, thanks, Mrs. Biggs," said Mark.

When Mark came back with the balloon, Katie was waiting. "Oh," she cried, "you got the balloon!"

Mark handed the balloon to Katie. "You and your witches, cat skins, and cauldrons!" he said. "You read too many fairy tales! Biggy's a nice little old lady, and now she's gone to the hospital."

"I'm sorry," said Katie, "but it all seemed pretty witchy to me. I'll make a get-well card for her."

"That's a good idea," said Mark, who was busy admiring the balloon.

"Oh, dear!" Katie moaned. "I did so hope that

we lived next door to a witch who would ride on a broomstick on Halloween. Just think, Markie, we would have been almost famous."

"Sometimes I think those fairy tales are making you nutty," said Mark.

Chapter 2

ANNA PATRICIA'S COSTUME

EDDIE WILSON and his friend Anna Patricia Wallace were in the same class in school. They were very good friends. Anna Patricia liked Eddie because he was always full of good ideas. Eddie liked Anna Patricia because she was always enthusiastic about his ideas. But sometimes Eddie thought Anna Patricia was a little nutty. She always had to tell him her secrets, and she had many secrets.

To Anna Patricia, Halloween was almost as important as Christmas. As soon as school started in September, Anna Patricia began to think about Halloween and what she would wear. By the first of October, she had imagined herself as a witch, as a cowgirl, as an angel, a ballet dancer, an evening star, and a Gypsy. She went to bed thinking about her costume and woke up thinking about it.

Each time she had a new idea she would tell Eddie about it. Eddie really didn't care what Anna Patricia wore with one exception. When she said she was going to be a cupid with a bow and arrow, he cried out, "A cupid! You'll catch a cold! Anyway, Annie Pat, it isn't Valentine's Day. It's Halloween." Eddie didn't want to go out on Halloween with a cupid.

Whenever Anna Patricia confided in Eddie, she would say, "Now, Eddie, remember this is a secret. You won't tell anyone, will you?"

"Oh, no!" Eddie would say. "I won't tell. But if I know you, Annie Pat, you'll be wearing something else when Halloween comes."

By the middle of October, Anna Patricia had changed her mind so many times that she couldn't remember what her first choice had been. But Anna Patricia didn't seem to care. Almost every morning she rushed up to Eddie and whispered, "Oh, Eddie! I have a wonderful idea for my Halloween costume! You'll keep it a secret if I tell you, won't you?"

One morning Eddie replied, "Annie Pat, I am stuffed so full of your secrets that they are coming out of my ears."

"Well," said Anna Patricia, "as long as they don't come out of your mouth, it's all right!"

Finally, a week before Halloween, Anna Patricia said to Eddie, "I have the best idea yet for my Halloween costume!"

"Good," said Eddie, "I hope you stick to it."

"Well, don't tell anybody, but I'm going to be a Spanish dancer, a flamenco dancer."

"Oh, yeah?" said Eddie, only half listening.

"And I'm going to have a tambourine, with all different colored ribbons. My mother borrowed it from a friend. It's beautiful," said Anna Patricia. "Are you listening to me, Eddie?"

"Sure, sure!" said Eddie. "Sounds great!"

That afternoon Eddie told his mother that he had decided to be a pirate on Halloween. He was going to wear a black mustache and a black patch over his eye. "I'll carry a knife between my teeth. I'll look real sharp."

"I hope the knife won't be sharp," said his mother. "I wouldn't want your mouth to be any bigger."

Eddie laughed. "Oh, Mom. I'll use a plastic knife," he said. Then he added, "Boodles and

Sidney and Annie Pat and I are going out trick or treating together. Annie Pat's finally decided she's going to be a flamingo."

"A flamingo?" said his mother. "How is she going to manage that?"

"I don't know," Eddie replied, "but she's crazy about the tambourine."

"She's going to be a bird with a tambourine! That's a new idea!" said Mrs. Wilson.

"Oh, no!" said Eddie. "She isn't going to be a bird! She's going to be a Spanish dancer."

"Oh!" said his mother. "The word is *flamenco*. not *flamingo*."

"Sounds like the same thing to me," said Eddie.

"Well, one happens to be a bird," said his mother, "and the other a Spanish dance."

Eddie laughed. "Well, this bird must be Spanish and dance with a tambourine."

Halloween night Eddie and his friends met at Sidney's house. All of them were very pleased with their costumes. Anna Patricia was wearing the Spanish dancer's dress and rattling the tambourine. Eddie had the patch over his eye and a plastic dagger between his teeth. His black mustache hung on each side of his mouth, a red sash of his mother's was tied around his middle, and a bright bandana was wound around his head. Boodles was wearing a terrible monster false face, with all-in-one pajamas that his mother had dyed green. Sidney was dressed as a clown. Her face was painted with a paste of flour and water, for her mother had forgotten to buy some white grease-paint.

Soon the four children set out. The first house they stopped at was where a teen-ager named Josie Jordan lived. There they found a Halloween party under way.

When Josie saw the children at the door, she called to her guests, "Oh, here are some Halloween kids. I'll ask them in. Let's see how good they are at bobbing for apples."

Josie pointed to the tub in the center of the room with apples bobbing around in the water.

One of the guests was Eddie's older brother Rudy. "Well, look who's here!" he said. "If it isn't my little brother and his pals! Do you kids want to see if you can catch an apple with your teeth? Betcha can't."

"Bet we can!" said Eddie, dropping down beside the tub.

"Sure we can," said Anna Patricia, hanging her head over the tub.

Everyone in the room stood watching the newcomers, who soon found out that catching an apple was not as easy as they had thought. The apples kept bobbing away just as their lips touched them. The spectators laughed.

"They're so slippery!" said Eddie.

Rudy and the others laughed.

Boodles tried to catch an apple while he was still wearing his false face, and he wondered why he couldn't open his mouth. But even when he took off his mask, he had trouble.

Sidney lifted her face out of the water and said, "I'll bet you big kids never caught one of these apples."

Now there were screams of laughter, for all the flour paste had washed off Sidney's face. She still had red lipstick on her lips and red spots on her cheeks, but her face was no longer white.

"Oh, look at Sidney," Eddie cried out. "She's lost her face."

Sidney looked in a mirror on the wall. "Oh, dear," she cried, "I'm all spoiled."

Josie's mother ran to the bathroom and came back with a box of white powder and a jar of vaseline. Quickly she put the vaseline on Sidney's face and dusted it with the powder. Soon Sidney looked more the way she had before her face floated away in the water.

Eddie and Anna Patricia continued to try to catch an apple. Suddenly Anna Patricia sat up and screamed. She pointed into the tub. "Oh," she cried, "there's a horrible spider in the tub."

Everyone stared at Anna Patricia in surprise. "Look, look!" she cried, pointing into the water. "It's a tarantula! A terrible tarantula!"

Rudy leaned over the tub, and then he scooped something out of the water. He held it up. "Look!" he said, "Eddie's lost his mustache. It's Anna Patricia's tarantula."

Everyone laughed harder than ever as Eddie wrung the water out of his mustache. "I guess I'll have to let it dry," he said. "I hope I can stick it back on."

Rudy said, "It doesn't look as though it will be dry before morning."

Anna Patricia went back to bobbing for apples, trying first one and then another. Suddenly she cried again, "Oh, I've lost my tooth. I've lost my tooth."

Anna Patricia had been losing her tooth from time to time, so nearly everyone knew about it. It was a little one that had been made to fit into a space where a tooth had been knocked out in an accident when she was little.

Now Anna Patricia ran to the mirror. "Oh, oh!" she cried. "I should have stuck to my first idea. Without my tooth, I look like a witch."

Eddie looked at Anna Patricia and said, "I don't know whether you're a witch or a flamingo, Annie Pat, but you sure are wet."

Anna Patricia tossed her curls and said, "Eddie Wilson, I am not a flamingo. I'm a flamenco dancer."

"Gwan," said Eddie, "you're a witch."

"Oh, wait a minute!" said Josie, as she ran out of the room. When she came back she had a black pointed witch's hat and a black cape. "I was a witch in a play once," she said, "and I still have the costume." Laughing, Josie put the black cape around Anna Patricia's shoulders and clapped the witch's hat on her head.

Eddie picked up a little broom that was resting

by the fireplace and handed it to Anna Patricia. "Here's your broom," he said. "Now let's see you fly." All of the children were laughing by this time.

Just then Josie's black cat walked into the room. Rudy picked it up and handed it to Anna Patricia. "Now you're a real witch," he said.

Anna Patricia joined in the laughter, but stopped as she remembered her tooth. "This is a lot of fun," she said, "but I have to find my tooth. I can't go to school tomorrow looking like a witch."

This time Josie's father came to the rescue. "So now we play Hunt the Tooth," he said, as he entered the living room.

"It must be in the tub, Daddy," said Josie.

"Yes!" said Eddie. "Unless she swallowed it."

"Oh, Eddie!" Anna Patricia cried. "Of course, I haven't swallowed it."

Just then Josie's mother came in with ice cream for all. "Well, here's something to swallow," she said.

The children ate the ice cream while they watched Mr. Jordan emptying the water out of the tub. He carried bucket after bucket out to the kitchen sink. At last the tub was empty, and Mr. Jordan held up Anna Patricia's tooth. "What am I offered for this fine tooth?" he asked.

Anna Patricia reached for it and said, "Oh, thank you." She pushed her tooth back where it belonged and picked up her tambourine. Then everyone laughed and clapped as they watched the witch in red shoes dancing around the room. As she danced she threw off the black cape, tossed the witch's hat to Eddie, and turned back into a Spanish flamenco dancer.

Now everyone's attention turned to Eddie and his mustache. It was still very damp. He tried to put it back on his upper lip, but it wouldn't stick.

Finally Rudy said, "Look, Eddie, you'll never get that to stick. I'll paint a mustache on your lip."

"But there won't be anything to hang down," said Eddie.

"Well, you can't have everything," said Rudy. "Every pirate didn't have a stringy mustache. Do you want me to paint it on or don't you?"

Reluctantly Eddie decided that a painted mustache would be better than no mustache, and he stood still while his brother did some art work on Eddie's upper lip with black poster paint.

When Rudy had finished, Eddie looked in the mirror, and he decided that his brother had done a very good job.

All the costumes were repaired now, so the party crashers were finally ready to continue their rounds. They thanked the Jordans for their help and left as everyone called good-by.

When the four children were outside, Eddie said, "Well, Annie Pat, I hope you aren't going to change your costume every time we stop. You made up your mind to be a flamingo, so now be a flamingo."

"Eddie Wilson!" said Anna Patricia, rattling her tambourine in his face. "How many times do I have to tell you? I'm not a bird. I'm a flamenco dancer."

Eddie flapped his arms like wings in reply. "Suit yourself, Annie Pat! You can dance with a tambourine, or you can fly. It's all the same to me. Just don't change your mind again!"

Chapter 3

THE TWO HALLOWEEN BEARS

PENNY WAS A LITTLE BOY. Patsy was a little girl. Both were exactly the same age. They lived next door to each other and were very good friends. They played together and went to school together on the school bus.

Both Penny and Patsy owned toy bears. They were their favorite toys. Both bears were named

Chocolate. They talked a great deal about "my Chocolate and your Chocolate."

As Halloween drew near, Penny and Patsy were invited to a Halloween party at Tommy Robbins's house. Everyone was going to dress in a costume and wear a false face. Penny and Patsy could hardly wait for the day to come.

The next afternoon, when the children were playing with their favorite toys in Patsy's play-room, Patsy said, "What are you going to wear to Tommy's party, Penny?"

Penny looked at their two toy bears, sitting beside each other, and he said, "I'm going to be a bear just like Chocolate. Why don't you be a bear too?"

"Oh!" said Patsy. "You mean twin bears? That would be fun. No one will know which is you and which is me."

"That's right!" said Penny. "We'll really fool them."

The children told their mothers that they

wanted to go to Tommy's party as twin bears, and their mothers agreed to make their bear costumes and to find bear false faces for them.

The week before Halloween Penny and Patsy went with their mothers to get their false faces. The man behind the counter in the shop went through a large drawer and soon found two bear false faces that were exactly alike. They were brown with hard black noses, and their red tongues were hanging out. When the children tried on the false faces, they agreed that they both looked very bearish, even though at the moment they were wearing plaid shirts and blue jeans.

Penny laughed and said, "When we get into our brown bear suits, we'll look like sure-enough bears."

"Sure will!" said Patsy.

When Halloween arrived, Patsy's mother brought Patsy, dressed in her bear suit, into Penny's house. Penny's mother had just finished zipping Penny into his brown fuzzy suit.

Their mothers laughed very hard as the children ran in and out of the room, for they couldn't tell which bear was Penny and which bear was Patsy. Penny's mother said, "You'll have a wonderful time at the party for everyone will get you mixed up. Think what fun it will be!"

When it was time to leave, Penny and Patsy asked if they could go by themselves. It wasn't very far, so their mothers agreed that they could walk over alone.

"But we will come for you," said Penny's mother. "We'll be there at nine o'clock."

"Okay!" said Penny, as the two bears went out the door.

They trotted down the street, and their mothers watched them until the children turned the corner. They couldn't tell which was Penny and which was Patsy.

As the children turned the corner, they came upon a great big police dog named Mike. Mike belonged to a neighbor, Mr. Turner. Penny and Patsy both loved Mike, and Mike was very fond of the children. But Mike didn't know the children, now that they were dressed like bears. To him they were just strange animals. He let out a low growl.

Penny and Patsy stood still. "Hello, Mike," said Penny. But the voice inside the false face didn't sound at all like Penny's voice.

Mike was sure he didn't like the strange animals now, so he gave a terrific bark.

"He doesn't know us," said Patsy. "Let's run home."

"No," said Penny. "He'll run after us, and he might catch us. Daddy always says you mustn't act scared."

The two bears huddled together against a stone wall. They were both trembling. "I'll go ring Mr. Turner's doorbell," said Patsy. "He'll come out and call Mike away."

Patsy rang the doorbell, but no one came to the door. "Oh, dear!" said Patsy. "Mr. Turner must be out somewhere."

"He goes out a lot on his motorcycle," said Penny. "I'll take off my false face, and perhaps Mike will leave us alone."

Penny laid his false face on the low stone wall. "See, Mike!" said Penny. "It isn't anything to be afraid of."

Mike barked and jumped up on the wall. He grabbed the bear's head by its nose. Then he jumped down and began to shake the false face very hard.

Penny called out, "Put it down, Mike! Put it down."

Mike did not put it down. He just shook it harder.

"Oh, dear!" Penny cried. "He'll tear it all up."

Mike seemed very pleased to have this enemy in his mouth. So in spite of Penny's cries of "Put it down! Put it down!" the dog started off on a run down the street, with the bear false face firmly in his mouth. Penny ran after Mike shouting, "Come back, Mike! Come back!"

Mike kept on running, and when he reached the corner he turned up the other street. Penny

chased him as fast as he could. Patsy trailed along behind.

Just as Penny was running out of breath, he heard the *chug, chug* of a motorcycle, and in a moment Mr. Turner on his motorcycle was coming toward Mike. Quickly Mr. Turner braked his motorcycle. Then he jumped off and went to catch Mike. To Penny's joy, Mr. Turner took the false face out of Mike's mouth.

Mr. Turner came toward Penny, holding out the false face. "Is this yours, Penny?" he asked.

"Oh, yes!" said Penny. "I guess we scared Mike. I guess he thought Patsy and I were real bears."

Mr. Turner put the false face on Penny and said, "I don't think he did any damage to this. You still look like a bear."

The children waited while Mr. Turner led Mike by his collar back to his house. Then Mr. Turner came back for his motorcycle. "Where are you two bears going?" he asked.

"We're going to Tommy Robbins's Halloween party, but I guess we're late now," said Penny.

"Well, Penny, you hop on the back seat of my motorcycle, and I'll take Patsy on the handlebars. I'll get you to the party in a jiffy."

As Mr. Turner chugged along, people stopped and laughed. Some children cried out, "Oh, look at those little bears, hugging the man on the motorcycle."

Mr. Turner let the children off at Tommy's house. There they rang the doorbell. They were surprised when the door was opened by Humpty Dumpty.

Humpty Dumpty led them down some stairs to a big cellar playroom. It was strung with strips of orange paper, and balloons bobbed against the ceiling. Ten children, dressed in Halloween costumes, were sitting quietly on the floor.

The two bears sat down beside each other just as Humpty Dumpty brought in a little boy carrying a candle. All of the children watched the boy as he put the candle down on the floor and jumped over it. Then the children shouted in a chorus:

"Jack be nimble, Jack be quick,
Jack jump over the candlestick."

Jack sat down beside the two bears.

Then Humpty Dumpty said, "Now we'll guess who everybody else is."

Penny knew at once that Humpty Dumpty was Tommy's daddy. He could tell from his deep voice.

It was great fun guessing who each child was. As each one was identified, he took off his mask. There was a great deal of laughing and shouting.

Finally everyone was unmasked but the two bears. And how Penny and Patsy giggled inside of their bear faces.

"I think they're Patsy and Penny," said a little witch.

"I'm sure they are," said Tommy the Indian. "But I don't know which is Penny and which is Patsy."

"Make them say something," said the cowboy. "We can tell by their voices."

"All right," said Mr. Robbins. "Say 'I'm a little brown bear.' "

Penny and Patsy each said, "I'm a little brown bear." But they sounded exactly alike. All of the children screamed with laughter.

Humpty Dumpty said they would have to give up. So the bears took off their faces, and Penny and Patsy each received a prize for the best Halloween costume.

The evening passed very quickly. The children played several games. Then they all sat down on the floor again and had ice cream and pretzels.

Just as Penny finished his ice cream he had an idea. He rushed over to Patsy and whispered something in her ear.

Patsy giggled. "Oh, yes, let's!" she said. "That will be fun!"

"What will be fun?" asked Sally, who was standing near.

"Oh, it's a secret," said Patsy.

"It isn't polite to have secrets at a party," said Sally.

"It isn't a secret about you," Patsy said. "It's something about our mothers."

When the two mothers arrived, the two little bears had their faces on again. They said good-by to Tommy and his mother and father and thanked them for a lovely party. Then they trotted home beside their mothers.

When they reached Penny's house, his mother said, "Say good-night to Patsy."

The children said good-night to each other and went in their houses. They were both still giggling.

"Run right upstairs now, Penny," said his

mother. "It's late. I'll help you out of your costume."

When they reached Penny's room, his mother sat down on the edge of his bed. She pulled the zipper and lifted the bear's face off. There, to her great surprise, was Patsy!

By this time Patsy was laughing so hard she fell back on the bed. She laughed and laughed.

Penny's mother laughed too. "Well, that was a surprise!" she said. "I wonder whether your mother has found out that she has the wrong bear."

In a few moments Patsy's mother came in with Penny. They were laughing too. "I would like to exchange this little bear," she said.

The two children couldn't stop laughing. "Oh, boy!" cried Penny. "Have we had fun. We fooled everybody!"

"Yes," shrieked Patsy with delight, "we fooled Mike too!"

"Best of all, we fooled our mothers," said Penny.

The children bounced with pleasure on the bed. "We fooled 'em! We fooled 'em!" It had been the best Halloween ever.

Chapter 4

MONKEY BUSINESS

IT WAS OCTOBER, and Halloween was drawing near. All the children were looking forward to the Halloween parade and the class parties. Of course, everyone was hoping to surprise everyone else, but it was hard for some of the children to keep secrets.

Eddie had no trouble deciding on his costume. He was going to be an organ-grinder. He already had the most important part of the costume, the organ, which he had bought at a second-hand shop long ago. What he needed was a monkey, and he didn't know where he could get one. He knew he couldn't buy a live one, and he didn't have a toy one. One day he decided to look for a toy monkey in the ten-cent store.

Eddie rode to the store on his bicycle. He locked his bike outside and went in the store. At the candy counter he bought himself a little bag of candy corn. Then he went to the toy counter. He looked over all the toys, but there was no monkey.

Eddie was just about to walk away, when he looked up at the Halloween masks that were hung on a heavy cord above the counter. As he raised his head, he stared right into the face of a monkey. It was a rubber mask made to fit over one's head. As Eddie looked up at the monkey face, he suddenly had one of his bright ideas. Sidney, the girl who lived next door to him, could be his monkey.

Eddie bought the mask and rode home. He could hardly wait to tell Sidney about his idea. As soon as he reached home, he shouted, "Hi, Sid!"

Sidney appeared at a side window. She beckoned Eddie to come in.

Eddie reached Sidney's front door just as she opened it. "Hi, Sid!" he said. "I have a wonderful idea for Halloween."

"I'm practicing my cello," said Sidney, "but come in. What's the idea?"

Eddie threw himself on the sofa, and Sidney sat on the floor beside her music stand. Her cello was resting against a chair.

"You know my hand organ," said Eddie.

"Sure!" said Sidney. "Do you want to trade it for something?"

"Nope," said Eddie. "I want a monkey to go with it."

"Swell!" said Sidney. "Where are you going to get one?"

"Right here!" said Eddie. He pounded on the sofa with his fist. "Right here."

"Are you crazy, Eddie?" said Sidney. "You know that I don't have a monkey."

"Look!" said Eddie, pulling the monkey mask out of his pocket. He put the mask over his head and pulled it down to cover his face.

Sidney jumped up. "Oh, Eddie!" she cried. "Are you going to be a monkey on Halloween, or an organ-grinder? You can't be both, can you?"

"I'm going to be the organ-grinder," replied Eddie. Then he pointed to Sidney and said, "You're going to be the monkey."

Sidney laughed and laughed. "Oh, Eddie!" she

gasped. "That's wonderful. Here, let me put it on right away."

Eddie took off the mask and handed it to Sidney. "We'll go into the parade together," said Eddie. "I have it all figured out. I'll grind my organ and have you on the end of a rope."

"And I'll carry a tin cup and tip my hat and dance around," said Sidney, pulling the mask down over her face. "How do I look?" she asked.

Eddie shouted with delight. "That's great!" he cried. "I can't wait for Halloween to come. We'll be the hit of the school parade."

Just then Sidney heard a car door slam. "Oh!" she cried. "Here comes my mother, and I haven't practiced my cello. You better go home, Eddie."

Eddie scooted out the back door.

Without thinking of the mask that she was wearing, Sidney picked up her cello. She placed it in front of her and began playing a sweet lullaby called "Sleep, Little One, Sleep."

Mrs. Stewart came in the front door with a big bag of groceries. She heard Sidney playing her cello. Sidney was playing very well. It was sweet music. Mrs. Stewart stopped at the living-room door to listen.

Sidney looked up at her mother and smiled sweetly, but her mother could not see Sidney's sweet smile. What she saw was the head of a monkey coming out of Sidney's blouse, which had a pink collar with white ruffles and a pink bow.

Mrs. Stewart dropped the whole bag of groceries. Apples, oranges, cans of soup, boxes of frozen vegetables, and a bag of dried lima beans went rolling all over the living-room floor. The bag of beans broke, and the beans flew everywhere.

The cello music stopped. "Oh, Mom!" cried Sidney. "What's the matter?"

"Oh, Sidney!" her mother cried. Mrs. Stewart began to laugh so hard she had to lean against the

wall. Then she sat down on the stairs and rocked back and forth.

Sidney couldn't believe that her mother was laughing about the groceries and beans that were all over the floor. She wondered whether her mother could be crying. She had never seen her mother cry. "I'll pick them up, Mommy. I'll pick them up!" said Sidney, dropping on her knees.

"Oh, Sidney!" her mother gasped. "You do look so funny. Where did you get that horrible mask?"

Now Sidney remembered that she was still wearing the monkey mask. She pulled it off. "Eddie gave it to me," she said laughing. "It's Eddie's idea. He's going to be an organ-grinder on Halloween, and I'm going to be his monkey."

When all the groceries and all the beans had been collected, Sidney said, "Will you make a costume for me, Mom?"

"Oh, yes! I'll make a monkey costume for you," her mother replied.

"Just like an organ-grinder's monkey?" Sidney asked.

"Yes," her mother said. "I'll make a short plaid kilt and a little red jacket with gold braid."

"And I have to have a little red hat, like a pillbox, with a strap under my chin," said Sidney.

"I can make that out of an old red-felt hat that's in the attic," said her mother.

"And I have to have a tail," said Sidney. "Can you make a tail?"

"I think I can make a tail," replied her mother.

Mrs. Stewart made Sidney a suit of dark-brown woolly material. It covered her from her feet to her neck. It had long sleeves that ended in fingers, like gloves. The suit was the monkey's skin. Sidney wanted a very long tail. It was made of the same brown material and was stuffed with cotton. "Sew it on very good, Mom," said Sidney, "so that nobody can pull it off."

Mrs. Stewart sewed it on with carpet thread. As

she pulled the needle through, she said, "No one will pull this tail off."

When the kilt and the red jacket were finished, and the red-felt hat fitted properly, Sidney could hardly wait for Halloween to come. Eddie was impatient too. His costume was ready. He had a large nose and long black mustachios to wear. His clothes would be brown baggy trousers, a checked shirt, and his father's old brown felt hat.

The day before Halloween Eddie and Sidney rehearsed their act in the Stewarts' living room. All went well. Sidney danced like a monkey on the end of Eddie's rope. She had a little trouble managing her tail. Once Eddie stepped on it, and Sidney cried, "Eddie, get off my tail!" No sooner had she spoken than she stepped on it herself and almost fell flat.

"Sid," said Eddie, "I think your tail is too long. You're going to have tail trouble, sure as shootin'."

"Oh, no! It's all right," said Sidney. "It's sewed on with carpet thread."

"Okay!" said Eddie. "We're going to roll 'em in the aisles tomorrow when we parade into the auditorium."

The following day all the children were excited about the Halloween parade and the parties. In the morning it was hard for them to think about their lessons.

Most of the children had brought their costumes with them, but Sidney's mother came for her at noon. She drove her home to put on the monkey costume. They were also bringing cupcakes and a jack-o'-lantern filled with peanuts back with them for the party.

When they returned, Mrs. Stewart parked the car by the curb in front of the school. "Can you manage these things, Sidney?" she asked. "If you can, I'll leave the car here and go do my marketing."

"Oh, yes!" said Sidney. "I'll take the cupcakes in and come back for the jack-o'-lantern."

"Very well," said her mother. "Just be sure you lock the car door when you finish unloading."

"All right!" said Sidney. "I'll remember."

Sidney's mother went off to do her marketing, and Sidney carried the box of cupcakes into the school. She carried her tail over her arm, like a train on a ball gown.

Inside the school there was a hum of children's voices coming from the open doors of the classrooms. Children in costumes scurried through the halls. On the way to her room, Sidney met a fairy, a bride, a red devil walking arm in arm with an angel, a canary bird sucking a lollipop, Red Riding Hood, and a butterfly having trouble with her garters.

When Sidney appeared in her classroom, all the children called out, "Oh, look at the monkey! Who's the monkey?"

Sidney whispered to Eddie, "I'll be back in a minute." She went back to the car for the jack-o'-lantern. This time, she forgot to hold her tail, and when she ran down the steps, it went bump-bump-bump-bump-bump all the way down.

Sidney opened the car door and stepped inside the car to get the jack-o'-lantern. It was on the back seat. She picked it up and stepped out of the car. Suddenly she remembered that her mother had told her to lock the car door, so she pushed down the little lock button on the door. She had the jack-o'-lantern in her left arm. With her right hand she slammed the door shut. Then she turned and started off. She took two steps, but on the third she was pulled back with a jerk. She looked behind her to see what was the matter. She soon found out. It was tail trouble, as Eddie had predicted. She had locked the door on her tail.

Sidney took hold of the handle of the door, hoping that it had not locked. But it was locked tight, and only the key would open it. The key was in her mother's purse.

Sidney looked around. There wasn't anyone in sight. It was very close to one o'clock, when the parade would start. Everyone was inside the school. She opened her mouth and yelled, "Help! Help! Help!"

No one appeared.

Inside the school the children were marching into the auditorium. Where is Sidney? thought Eddie. He couldn't go in without his monkey. Where had she gone? He went to the front door to see if he could find her. He opened the door. Then he heard someone calling, "Help! Help! Help!"

Eddie rested his hand organ against the steps and ran out to Sidney. "What's the matter?" he cried.

"My tail's caught in the door," said Sidney.

"Well, open the door," said Eddie.

"I can't. It's locked," said Sidney.

"I told you that tail was too long," said Eddie.

"Well, do something!" cried Sidney.

Eddie ran back into his classroom and returned with a pair of scissors. "Here!" he said. "I'll have to cut it off." He knelt down and started to hack off Sidney's tail. It was hard to cut the heavy cotton stuffing.

"Hurry up!" said Sidney.

"It's tough," said Eddie.

At last he cut through the tail, and Sidney was free. The organ-grinder and his monkey ran up the steps and through the door. Eddie picked up his hand organ and hooked a leash onto Sidney's belt. Now they were ready to follow the parade. When they reached the stage of the auditorium, everyone clapped.

Eddie ground out "The Band Played On," and Sidney danced. She danced just like an organ-grinder's monkey. She tipped her little red hat when Mr. Harris, the school principal, put a penny in her mother's measuring cup.

When Mrs. Stewart came back from her marketing, a black cocker spaniel was lying beside her car chewing on the remains of Sidney's tail. So, said Mrs. Stewart to herself, there must have been tail trouble!

At three o'clock, when all of the parties were over, Eddie's mother came for Eddie and Sidney and, of course, the hand organ. They drove away from the school and stopped for a red light at the corner.

Eddie was looking out the window while Sidney told Mrs. Wilson all about the parade and the parties. Suddenly Eddie cried out, "Look, Sid! There goes a cocker spaniel with the end of your tail!"

Chapter 5

TRICK OR TREAT

MR. TIMKIN was an elderly man who lived alone. He was a retired Navy man and had spent many years sailing all over the world under the United States flag.

Every day Eddie passed Mr. Timkin's house on his way to and from the school bus. On nice afternoons Mr. Timkin always sat on his front porch. At first Eddie and Mr. Timkin just waved to each other as Eddie went by. But after a while Eddie began to stop on his way home now and then to chat with Mr. Timkin. He liked to listen to the exciting stories that Mr. Timkin told about life on the sea and in strange faraway ports. One day Mr. Timkin taught Eddie how to fold a piece of paper and make an airplane. Soon Eddie and Mr. Timkin had become very good friends.

As Halloween drew near, Eddie made plans to go trick or treating once again with his friends Boodles and Anna Patricia and Sidney. On Halloween night, the four children, dressed in their Halloween costumes, met at Sidney's house. Eddie, of course, was a sailor, Boodles was a hobo, Sidney was a ballet dancer, and Anna Patricia was an Indian.

Anna Patricia, the great talker, said, "I'm really an Indian princess. My name is Mini-haha."

"Oh," said Eddie, who liked nothing better than to tease Anna Patricia, "so you're a little ha ha. I guess that means we'll be laughing a lot tonight."

Anna Patricia tossed her head and rattled her strings of beads. "I am an Indian princess," she repeated with great dignity.

"Well, Haha!" said Eddie. "Let's get moving along. We need lots of time if we're going to get any treats and do any tricks."

"Come along, Haha!" said Boodles, as he opened the door.

The four children went outside. Each one had a shopping bag for candy and a UNICEF box for pennies.

"Now," said Sidney, "where shall we go?"

"Wherever we go," said Boodles, "I hope we get some peanut bars. I sure like peanut bars!"

"Boodles!" said Anna Patricia. "Don't you ever think about anything but candy?"

TRICK
OR
TREAT

"Sure, Haha!" said Boodles. "Sometimes I think about ice cream."

"Look," said Eddie, "are you and little Haha going trick or treating or are you just going to stand there talking about food? We'll never get anything if we don't go soon. Remember, we're not the only kids out tonight."

"Where shall we go first?" Sidney asked.

"Let's go to Mr. Timkin's," said Eddie. "He's a friend of mine. He was a Navy man."

"Oh, I know who Mr. Timkin is," said Sidney. "I see him sitting on his porch. He always waves to me."

"Okay, Eddie!" said Boodles. "Is that why you're dressed up like a sailor? I hope he won't give us hardtack or bully beef."

"What's that?" Anna Patricia asked.

Boodles laughed and said, "It's the grub that sailors always get in sea stories, and it doesn't sound as good as peanut bars!"

Eddie led the way to Mr. Timkin's house.

They climbed the steps onto the porch, and Eddie rang the bell. Soon footsteps sounded inside the house.

"He's coming!" said Anna Patricia.

"Yeah, I sure hope he has peanut bars for us," said Boodles.

In a moment, the porch light was turned on, the door opened, and Mr. Timkin appeared in his bathrobe. When he saw the children, he cried, "Oh, Halloween! I forgot all about it! Seems I can't keep track of the days. Being all alone, there's nobody here to tell me. Probably miss Christmas if somebody doesn't tell me in time." Then he threw up his hands and said, "I haven't a thing to put in your bags. I'm sorry."

"That's all right," Sidney said. "Do you have any pennies for our UNICEF boxes instead?"

Mr. Timkin felt in his pockets. "Not a cent," he said. "Not a cent to put in your boxes. I just forgot about Halloween. I'll do better next year if someone will just tell me."

Then Mr. Timkin held his hand out to Eddie and said, "I'm glad you've joined the Navy, Eddie."

"Sure!" said Eddie. "Someday I'll be Admiral Edward Wilson."

"Says you!" said Anna Patricia.

"Haha," said Eddie, "I'll be an admiral before you'll be an Indian."

Mr. Timkin laughed and closed the door.

As the children left the porch, Anna Patricia said, "Now we have to play a trick."

"Yes, a trick!" said Boodles and Sidney.

"He just forgot," said Eddie. "If he had remembered, he would have had something ready for us."

"That isn't any excuse," said Anna Patricia. "If I forgot to do my homework, I wouldn't be forgiven and neither would you, Eddie."

"I know a good trick," said Sidney. "My cousin told me about it."

"Well, what is it?" said Boodles.

"You take the gate from the fence and hide it. It's a great trick."

"Let's do that!" Anna Patricia cried.

Eddie looked out toward the street. "I don't see how we can take his gate away, when he doesn't even have a fence."

"Oh!" exclaimed Eddie's three friends.

"We'll think of something else," said Anna Patricia.

"We could upset his rubbish cans," said Sidney. "That's another good trick."

"Great!" said Anna Patricia. "Let's do that."

"We'll have to find the rubbish first," said Boodles, as they all ran off the porch.

They went completely around the house, but they couldn't find any rubbish cans.

"Oh, shucks!" said Sidney. "Rubbish must be in the garage."

"Too neat!" said Anna Patricia. "That's what this guy is, too neat."

"I know a good trick," said Boodles.

"What is it?" asked Anna Patricia.

"You push the doorbell," said Boodles, "and then you put a pin in it. The doorbell goes on ringing and ringing. It's a good trick."

Anna Patricia squealed. "Let's do it!" she cried. "It sounds great. Who has a pin?"

"Not me," said Sidney.

"Gee!" said Boodles. "I thought girls always had pins. How about you, Eddie? Do you have a pin?"

"What would I be doing with a pin?" Eddie answered. "Sailors don't carry pins."

Anna Patricia pointed to Boodles' tattered jacket and said, "You look as though you were put together with pins, Hobo. Can't you find one?"

Boodles looked at the lapel of his old jacket. "What do you know?" he cried. "Here's a pin."

The children ran up to the front door, and Sidney pushed the doorbell button as Boodles put the pin in the crack. "Beat it now!" he said to his friends. "Beat it!"

The children ran off the porch and down the steps. At the foot of the steps, Anna Patricia tripped and fell. When she hit the ground, one of her strings of beads broke and the beads scattered all over the ground. As Eddie helped her up, Anna Patricia cried, "Oh, no! I've broken my mother's string of beads, and I'll never find them in the dark. Oh, what will I do?"

Just then Mr. Timkin answered the ringing bell. "What's the matter out here?" he called.

"Anna Patricia fell down," said Eddie.

"Oh, did she hurt herself?" Mr. Timkin asked.

"No," said Eddie, as loud as he could above the ringing bell. "She just broke her mother's beads."

"Eddie Wilson!" cried Anna Patricia. "How do you know I didn't hurt myself? My leg hurts. Maybe I broke it."

"You're standing on your legs," said Eddie, "so I don't think you broke it."

"Well, I broke my mother's beads," said Anna Patricia, "and I can't find them."

Then Mr. Timkin said, "If I can stop this blankety-blank bell from ringing, I'll get a flashlight and I'll help the little girl find her beads."

As the children watched guiltily, Mr. Timkin examined the doorbell and easily pulled out the pin. Now there was quiet again. Without saying a word, he disappeared and soon was back with the flashlight and a paper bag. He flashed the light all around and helped the children hunt for the beads. As they found them they put them into the paper bag.

When all of the beads were recovered, Anna Patricia said, "Oh, thank you, Mr. Timkin. I never could have found them without your flashlight."

"Glad to help!" Mr. Timkin was laughing as he looked at the children. "That was a good trick you played on me. I used to stick pins in bells when I was a kid too. Serves me right for not having anything for you on Halloween. But you come back later. I'll see if I can find something in my freezer. Maybe I have something there that I can give you."

"We'll be back, Mr. Timkin," said Eddie. "Come on," he called to his friends, "we better go see what stuff is left."

The children needed no urging, and they quickly ran off to make more calls. All of them were uneventful, and they gathered their treats without any further problem. About an hour later, they were back on Mr. Timkin's porch. Boodles rang the bell, but this time he did not put a pin in it.

A few moments later Mr. Timkin opened the door. "Well now," he said, "if you children will come into the house, I think I have something for you."

The children entered the house, and Mr. Timkin led them to the kitchen. On the table there was a beautiful chocolate cake covered with chocolate icing and decorated with nuts. Mr. Timkin pointed to the cake and said, "My daughter baked that for me some time ago. I decided to put it into the freezer and keep it for some special occasion, and tonight is a very special occasion."

Soon Mr. Timkin had cocoa ready to pour into five mugs. Then he cut five large pieces of cake, and the children sat down to a real party. At last Mr. Timkin said, "Must be nearly your bedtime."

"Guess so!" the children agreed.

"It's been a wonderful Halloween!" said Anna Patricia.

"Best chocolate cake I ever ate," said Boodles.

"It was a great Halloween!" said Sidney. "Thanks for the treat."

When Eddie thanked Mr. Timkin, he saluted him, and Mr. Timkin returned Eddie's salute with a flourish.

Outside Anna Patricia said, "I'm glad we didn't

play a bad trick on Mr. Timkin. He's such a nice man."

"He's a great guy!" said Eddie. "I wish I could have served on the same ship with him."

Chapter 6

BILLY'S HALLOWEEN PARTY

IT WAS HALLOWEEN, and Betsy was dressing for a party. Billy Porter, who was in Betsy's class in school, was giving the party.

On Betsy's bed sat Betsy's little sister, Star, dressed as a dwarf with a long gray beard. She was wearing dark-green breeches and a black velvet jacket. On her head was a pointed hat, and her brown shoes had long pointed toes that turned up at the ends. The dwarf's face was very sad. Every few minutes she would sob and then sniffle. Sob-sniffle! Sob-sniffle! went the dwarf.

Finally Betsy said, "Oh, Star, don't cry. You'll be invited to a party when you're bigger. You're only five years old."

"I want to go to a party now," said Star. "I'm all dressed up for Halloween, and I can't go to a party."

"But there are plenty of kids who aren't going to the party," said Betsy. "Even Eddie Wilson isn't going to the party, and he's eight years old."

Betsy was putting on her costume. She put on a long black skirt and a black cape. Then she put a tall, pointed black hat on her head. When she put on her false face, she looked horrible. Now she truly seemed to be an old witch with a hooked nose and a grinning mouth with only one tooth. The minute Betsy turned and faced Star, the dwarf leaped from the bed and ran out of the room screaming loudly.

"What's the matter?" asked Mother, as Star ran into her in the hall.

"It's Betsy!" cried Star. "She's an old witch!"

Betsy laughed behind her false face. "Don't I look wonderful, Mother?" she said.

"You certainly look horrible," said Mother.

Now that Star had hold of her mother's hand she wasn't afraid. "You're going to scare everybody at the party, Betsy," she said. She began to wish once more that she could go too. "I wish I could go to the party and see you scare everybody," she said.

"Father is going to pick up your friend Lillybell, and he'll take you both around trick or treating," said Mother.

Just then Eddie Wilson's father drove up in his car. On the back seat were the ten-year-old Wilson twins, Joe and Frank, and another boy and girl. All of them were dressed in their Halloween costumes. They were on their way to Billy's party.

When Betsy came out of the house to get into the car, Joe cried, "Oh, look at the old witch!"

Betsy climbed into the front seat beside Mr. Wilson.

"Oh, Betsy!" cried Frank. "Eddie's mad because he wasn't invited to the party."

"Isn't he going to get dressed up?" Betsy asked.

"He wouldn't tell," said Joe. "He just kept saying he'd show everybody. He'd scare everybody stiff."

All the children shouted gleefully. "I'd like to see him scare me," said Joe.

"Me too," said Frank.

In the meantime, Star's father drove her around to Lillybell's house. Lillybell was dressed like a bride. She was wearing a long white dress, and her mother had fastened a piece of an old lace curtain on her head. She had on white gloves and carried a bunch of white-paper flowers. Her false face had long curly eyelashes, which Lillybell thought were very beautiful.

When the little dwarf and the bride were both settled in the car, Star's father said, "How about calling on Mrs. Wilson and Eddie?"

"Eddie's mad because he can't go to Billy's party," said Star.

"Well, perhaps we can cheer him up," said her father.

When they reached the Wilsons' house, Star and Lillybell went by themselves to the front door and knocked. They waited and knocked again a little louder.

At last they heard footsteps. The door was opened with a swish by what looked to Star and Lillybell like a flock of ghosts, led by a horrible white skeleton.

"Oh, oh, oh!" they shrieked. Star raced back to the car, followed by Lillybell, tripping all the way over her long white dress.

"Hey!" shouted the voice of little Eddie Wilson. "Hey, wait!"

Star was kneeling on the seat of the car with her face hidden against her father's shoulder. Lillybell was hiding her face against Star's back.

"Hey!" cried Eddie, as he reached the car. "They're just balloons. Come on in. I need you."

Star heard her father laugh, so she turned and peeked out between her fingers at Eddie.

Eddie was standing by the car, holding three balloons. Two were white with eyes and nose and mouth painted on them with black paint. Each balloon was draped in a white cheesecloth duster. With the moonlight shining on them and the wind blowing the white dusters, they looked like very scary ghosts. The other balloon was black. It had a white skeleton painted on it.

"I'm going to the party at Billy Porter's," said Eddie, "and I'm going to scare the crowd out of their wits. Only I have to have somebody to help me."

"I'll help you," said six-year-old Lillybell. But she spoke in a very small voice, because she was still a little bit scared.

"I'll help you too," said Star.

"Well," said Eddie, "I guess there isn't anybody else."

Then Eddie looked at Star's father and said, "Please, will you take me over to Billy Porter's house? I'd 'preciate it a lot."

"Well," said Star's father, "I guess if you can't play pranks on Halloween, it isn't Halloween. If your parents don't mind, come along."

Eddie went back to the house to tell Mr. and Mrs. Wilson where he was going. In a minute he reappeared and climbed into the back seat of the car with his balloons. Star and Lillybell sat on the front seat.

On the way to Billy's house, Eddie told them his plan. "The party is going to be in the Porters' living room," said Eddie. "I've cased the place."

"What did you do to the place?" Lillybell asked.

"I cased it," said Eddie.

"What's that?" said Star.

"That means I've looked the place over, found out where the windows are," said Eddie. "When you are a detective, you say you've cased the place."

"Oh," said Lillybell. "You mean you're a snooper."

"Well, you gotta snoop if you want to scare people on Halloween," said Eddie, "and we're gonna scare this crowd."

"Are we snoopers?" asked Star.

"You bet," Eddie replied. "Snoopy snoopers! That's us!"

The little girls giggled, for they were having fun.

"Now," said Eddie, "the living room has three windows, and I'm going to scare them at all three, but I can't do it by myself." Then Eddie told Star and Lillybell what they were to do. When he finished he said, "Now do you understand?"

"Oh, yes!" said the bride and the dwarf together.

When they reached Billy Porter's house, they got out of the car. Eddie handed both Star and Lillybell a ghost balloon.

Star's father tied each little girl's balloon to her wrist. "Now take hold of the string, close to the balloon," he said. "And remember, when you get under the window, let go of the string. Then the balloon will float up so it can be seen. It won't get away from you, because the end of the string is tied to your wrist."

"I know how to do it," said Star, as she tiptoed toward the house.

"Sh!" said Eddie. "Don't let them go until you hear me tap on the window."

"Okay," said Lillybell.

The children were very close to the house now. They could hear the boys and girls inside shouting and laughing. They sounded as though they were having a good time. Suddenly all the lights went out. The children in the house shrieked. Someone inside the house was trying to scare them too. It was a perfect time for Eddie's trick.

At this moment Star and Lillybell and Eddie were each crouching below one of the living-room windows. Star's father was beside her.

Eddie reached up and tapped on the window. Immediately the three balloons bobbed up. A full moon cast an eerie light and wind whipped the cheesecloth dusters, as Eddie pulled his skeleton up and down.

"Look, look!" someone inside cried out.

"Oh, oh! Eeek!" Wild cries came from the inside of the house.

Eddie and Star and Lillybell laughed and laughed and so did Star's father.

"That scared 'em," said Eddie.

In a few minutes the front door was opened, and Mr. Porter looked out. When he saw who was outside, he called, "Come in, Ghosties. You've just about scared this crowd stiff."

"I told you I would," said Eddie, as he walked into the house.

When Betsy saw Star and Lillybell, she said, "How did you babies get into this?"

"We came to help Eddie scare you," said Lillybell.

And just then Mrs. Porter began serving ice cream.

The dwarf fell sound asleep on her father's lap before she had finished hers. Mr. Porter had to carry Lillybell out to the car. She, too, was sound asleep. The ghost balloons were still tied to the wrists of the dwarf with the long gray beard and the bride with the curly eyelashes.

Chapter 7

JONATHAN AND THE JACK-O'-LANTERN

JONATHAN MASON was six years old. He used to live on the edge of a big city, but now he lived far out in the country. His father wrote books and liked to be where it was quiet, so he had found a nice farmhouse for the family. A farmer named Mr. Tattersall, who lived nearby, was happy to farm the land that Jonathan's father had bought with the house.

Mr. Tattersall and Jonathan soon became very good friends. Jonathan liked to watch Mr. Tattersall on the farm. He liked to see him plough the fields with his horses.

One spring day Jonathan noticed Mr. Tattersall kneeling beside the vegetable garden. Jonathan ran to find out what the farmer was doing. When Mr. Tattersall saw Jonathan coming toward him, he said, "Morning, Jonathan! I'm getting the seeds in."

Jonathan stood beside Mr. Tattersall. "What kind of seeds are you planting today?"

"I'm putting in the pumpkins," Mr. Tattersall replied.

"Oh!" said Jonathan. "When Halloween comes, my daddy makes a jack-o'-lantern for me."

"Don't say!" said Mr. Tattersall. "How be if

your father uses one of these pumpkins this year?"

"I'd like that," said Jonathan.

So Jonathan came every day to see how the pumpkins were growing. When he saw the first green sprouts, he was very excited. He announced the news on the school bus to Mr. Riley the bus driver, whom all the children called Rus. And to every child who boarded the bus, he said, "Mr. Tattersall is growing a pumpkin for me. It's going to be my jack-o'-lantern next Halloween."

Jonathan looked at the pumpkins every day all during the summer. By the time October arrived, they were nice and fat and round.

From the bus windows, Jonathan watched the leaves falling like golden showers from the trees. He saw the corn shocks that the farmers had gathered from the cornfields. Some of the corn shocks had bright orange pumpkins nestled beside them.

Suddenly, through the window, Jonathan saw

something very strange. "Oh, Rus! Look!" he called out.

Mr. Riley was so surprised that he slowed down. "What is it?" he asked.

"Over there!" said Jonathan. "Sitting on that chair with a jack-o'-lantern head. It's all dressed up."

Mr. Riley looked and said, "Oh, that's one of the Pumpkin People. They always come out around Halloween time. You'll see more of them."

Sure enough! Not much farther on, Jonathan called out, "There are three more Pumpkin People."

"Yes," said Mr. Riley. "A whole family, sitting on chairs. Mr. and Mrs. Pumpkin and little Peter Pumpkin."

"What are they made of?" asked Jonathan.

"Oh, you stuff an old suit to make Mr. Pumpkin and an old dress for Mrs. Pumpkin and a little boy's suit for Peter Pumpkin."

"What do people stuff them with?" asked Jonathan.

"Often as not, it's hay or just old newspapers," said Mr. Riley.

When Jonathan reached home, he rushed into the house calling out, "Mommy, Mommy! The Pumpkin People are out!"

"Who is out, Jon?" his mother asked.

"The Pumpkin People," said Jonathan.

"Now who are the Pumpkin People?" she replied.

Jonathan told his mother about the Pumpkin People he had seen. "They have heads that look just like the jack-o'-lantern Daddy makes for me at Halloween."

"Well, I'll have to look for these new neighbors," said Mrs. Mason.

The week before Halloween the children began to talk about the Halloween parade. Jonathan had never been in one or even seen one. In the

big city his father had taken him to see the Thanksgiving parade, and once he had seen the Saint Patrick's Day parade. But a Halloween parade was something new.

Jonathan's friend Melissa told him all about it. "Everybody gets all dressed up," she said. "I'm going to be a fairy. What are you going to be, Jon?"

"I don't know," Jonathan replied.

"There's a prize for the best costume," said Melissa. "Each room gets a prize. The parents come, and they decide. My cousin Marcie won one last year."

"What was the prize?" Jonathan asked.

"It was a book, with lots of colored pictures," said Melissa.

"Oh, I like books!" said Jonathan. "I'd like to win a book."

"Then you'll have to think up a good costume," said Melissa.

"Where do they have the parade?" Jonathan asked.

"Last year we went outside, 'cause it wasn't cold," said Melissa. "But if it's cold, we'll have it all around, inside the school."

Several days before Halloween Jonathan said to his mother, "Mr. Tattersall said he'd give us a good pumpkin for the jack-o'-lantern."

"We can go and get one right now," his mother replied. "Mr. Tattersall has a lot of pumpkins. He gathered them all out of the field, and he told me we could help ourselves."

It was chilly outside, so Jonathan and his mother buttoned up their coats. They walked up the lane until they came to Mr. Tattersall's house. He was outside, burning a pile of leaves. When he saw his visitors, he called out, "How do, Mrs. Mason! How do, Jonathan."

Mr. Tattersall led Jonathan and his mother to a large pile of bright golden pumpkins. He picked up one. Jonathan noticed that it was swollen on one side, and he hoped that he would not have to take it. He didn't want his jack-o'-lantern to look as though it had a toothache.

Jonathan gave a sigh of relief when Mr. Tattersall put it back on the pile. "Guess that won't do," he said. Anxiously Jonathan watched as Mr. Tattersall went through the rest of the pile. At last, he picked up a big round pumpkin. "How's this?" he asked, holding it up.

"Oh, that's a good one!" Jonathan exclaimed. "That will make a wonderful jack-o'-lantern."

Mr. Tattersall put the pumpkin into Jonathan's arms. It was so big that Jonathan couldn't carry it, so he gave it to his mother to bring home. "Thank you, Mr. Tattersall," he said.

On the way back, Jonathan said to his mother, "I can't wait to see this jack-o'-lantern."

Halloween was very near now, but Jonathan still had not decided what costume to wear in the parade. His mother made many suggestions. He could be a clown or a sailor or a soldier, but Jonathan didn't care for any of these ideas.

"I want to be different from everyone else," he said.

Then one day, while he was looking out the window of the bus, he knew what he wanted to be. When he reached home, he rushed into the house and called out, "Mommy, I know what I want to be in the parade!"

"Good!" said his mother. "Tell me."

"I want to be a Pumpkin Person! A Pumpkin Man!"

"How will you manage that?" his mother asked.

"I'll wear some old clothes and put the jack-o'-lantern on my head. It will be much better than one of those old false faces."

"But how can you get your head inside the pumpkin, Jon?" his mother said.

"I'll get Daddy to cut a hole in the bottom of

the jack-o'-lantern," he answered. "I can see out of the jack-o'-lantern's eyes. Daddy will help me."

Jonathan was right. Mr. Mason laughed and promised to carve the jack-o'-lantern for him to wear.

The night before Halloween, as soon as dinner was over, Mr. Mason seated himself at the kitchen table and started to carve the pumpkin. Jonathan sat on a stool beside him, so he could watch the pumpkin turn into a jack-o'-lantern. After Mr. Mason had cut a large piece out of the bottom of the pumpkin, he scraped out the seeds and pulp until the pumpkin was just an empty shell. Then with a sharp knife he cut out two triangular holes for the eyes and another one for the nose. Mr. Mason took a long time to cut out the mouth, but it was a nice smiling one when he finished.

"Now we'll try it on, Jon," said his father.

But when Mr. Mason put the pumpkin over

Jonathan's head, it only went down as far as his ears. It looked very funny, for the jack-o'-lantern's mouth was up as far as Jonathan's forehead.

"I'll have to make that hole bigger," said Jonathan's father.

Mr. Mason cut the hole bigger several times. Each time Jonathan tried the jack-o'-lantern on until it finally covered his whole head and he could look out through the eyeholes. When he examined himself in the mirror, he was delighted. "Oh!" he cried, "I do look like a Pumpkin Person."

His mother laughed. "You sound as though you were talking under the bedclothes," she said.

"You should sit outside on the front porch," said his father.

Jonathan laughed. "Oh, no!" he said, "I'm going to be in the parade!" Suddenly he looked at himself again. "Daddy, the Pumpkin Person doesn't have any teeth!"

"That's because he's very young," said his father. "Just born, you know. No teeth!"

Jonathan laughed. "He'll get some teeth, won't he, Daddy?"

"Oh, sure!" said his father. "I'm a good dentist. Just call me Dr. Mason. I'll give him teeth." Mr. Mason picked up some of the pumpkin seeds and put them in the jack-o'-lantern's mouth.

Jonathan laughed and said, "Oh, he looks great! I think he's the nicest jack-o'-lantern I ever had."

The following morning Jonathan got dressed for the Halloween parade. He put on his oldest pair of jeans, which had a big patch on one knee. Then he got out an old, faded plaid shirt. It was a little too small for him, but that didn't matter. Last he put on his sneakers, the ones with holes in the toes. Now he looked just like a Pumpkin Person, all except for his head.

When Jonathan went down to breakfast, his mother said, "Jon, I don't think you'll be able to manage that big pumpkin on the school bus. I'll drive you to school this morning."

Jonathan put on his jack-o'-lantern when he got in the car. He rode to school wearing the

pumpkin. It had a nice Halloween pumpkin smell.

When Jonathan walked into school, the children cried out, "Oh, look at the Pumpkin Person! Who do you think it is?"

Jonathan didn't say a word as the children gathered around him. They all tried to guess who the Pumpkin Person was.

Finally Melissa said, "Jon wasn't on the bus this morning. I think it must be Jon."

"Yes! Yes!" the children cried. "Bet it's Jon."

Melissa went up to Jon and peeked into the mouth of the jack-o'-lantern. "It's Jon!" she cried, jumping up and down. "I can see him inside."

The children laughed and called out, "It's Jon! It's Jon!"

When Jonathan's teacher, Miss Adams, arrived, Jonathan took off his pumpkin and put it in the corner at the back of the room.

At lunchtime, the children formed for the parade. Jonathan's class joined the rest of the

school in the big hall. Everyone was in costume, and they looked very festive. There were Gypsies, ghosts, monsters, fairies, soldiers, sailors, football players, rabbits, ballet dancers, and even a Jack-in-the-box.

As it was a sunny October day, the parade marched all around the school yard. Parents and teachers had gathered to watch, and they clapped whenever an especially clever costume went by.

When the parade was over, Miss Adams said, "The prize for our room will be awarded after you have had your lunch."

All through lunch the children chattered about the parade and who would win the prize.

When they returned to their classroom, Miss Adams said, "The parents have voted, and now

Adams. All the children looked expectantly at her. With a smile, she said, "Jonathan has won the prize."

Jonathan exclaimed, "You mean me?"

"Yes, Jonathan," said Miss Adams, "you have won the prize for the most original costume."

All the children clapped as Jonathan walked to the front of the room. He was very surprised when Miss Adams picked up the old gray cardboard box. Could it be a prize? This old gray box! Miss Adams held it out toward Jonathan, so he reached up and took it.

"I hope you will like it, Jon," said Miss Adams.

Jonathan looked into the box and cried out excitedly, "Oh! Oh!" There in the bottom of the box was a pale gray kitten.

"What is it, Jon? What is it?" the children called to him.

Jon lifted the kitten out of the box and held it in his arms. His face was covered with a smile. He cuddled the kitten against his cheek.

The children crowded around Jonathan to pet the kitten.

"What are you going to name it?" Melissa asked.

Jonathan thought a moment. "I'm going to name him after my jack-o'-lantern," he said. "His name is Jackie."

Jonathan's mother drove him home from school, and again Jonathan wore his pumpkin head in the car. This trip, though, he held a gray cardboard box in his lap.

When they reached home, his mother said, "Your head must be very hot inside that jack-o'-lantern. I'm sure you'll be glad to take it off."

"Yes, but you know, Mommy, it's fun wearing it," said Jonathan.

They walked into the kitchen, and Jonathan leaned over to put the box with the kitten in it down on the floor. As he bent down, the jack-o'-lantern bumped against an open cupboard door and the pumpkin fell in pieces on the floor.

"Oh!" cried Jonathan. "Oh, my jack-o'-lantern!"

"Never mind," said his mother. "Jack may be gone, but you still have Jackie!"

Chapter 8

WHO SCARED WHO?

IT WAS THE WEEK before Halloween. Donald and Ronald, the four-year-old twins, were looking in a shopwindow. The window was filled with false faces—funny false faces, ugly false faces, pretty false faces. Granny stood beside the children while they pointed to the ones they liked the best.

"I like the ugly ones," said Donald.

"I do too," said Ronald.

"Can I have an ugly face, Granny, and go out and scare everybody?" Ronald asked.

"Oh, I don't think you want to go out and scare people," said Granny.

"Yes!" cried both twins. "We'll scare 'em." Jumping up and down, the twins shouted, "We'll scare 'em! We'll scare 'em!"

"Who are you going to scare?" asked Granny.

"Everybody," said Donald.

"Even the policemen, Mr. Kilpatrick and Mr. McGillicuddy," said Ronald.

"Oh, I don't think you could scare the policemen," said Granny.

"If we were ugly enough, we could," said Donald.

"Granny, can't we buy our false faces now?" asked Ronald.

"Well, we might as well do it and get it over," said Granny.

Granny and the twins went into the store. The man behind the counter said, "Good afternoon, what can I do for you?"

"We're looking for false faces," said Granny.

"Ugly ones," said Ronald.

"Yes," said Donald. "We're going to scare Mr. Kilpatrick and Mr. McGillicuddy."

"Well, let's see," said the shopkeeper, as he went through a pile of false faces. "What about this?" He handed a false face over the counter to Granny.

"Let's see! Let's see!" shouted the twins.

Granny held it up to her face and looked down at the twins. It was the face of a witch.

"It isn't ugly enough," said Donald.

"Want an ugly one," said Ronald.

The shopkeeper went through another pile of false faces. "Well, what about this?" he said, handing Granny another.

Granny held it up to her face and looked down at the two little boys. It was certainly an ugly false face. The mouth was crooked, the nose was crooked, and there was a black patch over one eye. It was the face of a pirate.

"Oh, that's a ugly face," said Ronald.

"Yes," said Donald, "it's ugly."

"Very well," said Granny. "We'll take two of these."

The shopkeeper went through the pile of false faces, looking for another one exactly like the one Granny held in her hand. Finally he said, "I'm afraid that's the only one I have."

The little boys looked as though they were going to cry. Then the shopkeeper reached into a showcase and picked up a limp piece of rubber. "Maybe they would like these," he said. "They're made of rubber and go right over your whole head. I have a lot of these."

The man put the rubber mask on, and then he leaned over the counter and looked down at the twins. Both the boys jumped. They ran to Granny and hid their faces against her.

The shopkeeper laughed. "Ha, ha!" he said. "That scared you. I guess that's ugly enough."

It was not exactly an ugly face, but it certainly was surprising. Instead of being pink, it was bright green. The nose was big and lumpy, the eyes bulged and were bright purple, the crooked mouth grinned to show one tooth, and the hair was like gray seaweed. It was queer enough to make anyone jump.

"See!" said Granny. "You don't want a face that will scare people. Look how scared you are."

"I'm not scared," said Donald, lifting his face out of Granny's skirt. "I like it."

"I like it too," said Ronald, peeking out between his fingers that covered his face.

The shopkeeper took off his mask. "It's what they call a troll," he said.

"What's a troll?" said Donald.

"It's a kind of dwarf," said Granny.

"I want to put it on," said Ronald.

The man came out from behind the counter and put the mask over Ronald's head. But when Ronald turned around, Donald let out a scream and ran to Granny again.

Ronald ran around the shop. Suddenly he caught sight of himself in a mirror. He was so surprised that he jumped. Then he cried, "Take it off! Take it off!"

Granny pulled the mask off. "Now, see!" she said. "You don't like being a troll."

"But it would scare Mr. Kilpatrick," said Ronald, after the mask was off.

"Yes, it would scare Mr. McGillicuddy," said Donald.

"But you're both afraid to wear it."

"I'm not afraid if I don't look at it," said Ronald.

"I'm not afraid of it," said Donald. "Please buy them, Granny."

"Very well," said Granny. Then she said to the shopkeeper, "We'll take two."

The shopkeeper picked out two rubber masks that were exactly alike. He put them in a paper bag and handed them to Granny.

About five o'clock every day Mr. Kilpatrick drove past the twins' house on his way home. Sometimes Mr. McGillicuddy was with him. Donald and Ronald always watched for Mr. Kilpatrick, for he stopped his car every time to talk to the little boys.

As soon as the twins had bought their false faces, they waited to see Mr. Kilpatrick. They rode their tricycles up and down the front pavement. Finally they saw the red car turn the corner. They pedaled as fast as they could toward the car, calling out, "Here comes Mr. Kilpatrick! Here comes Mr. Kilpatrick!"

Mr. Kilpatrick stopped the car, and the twins rode up beside it. Mr. McGillicuddy was there too.

"Hello, Mr. Kilpatrick!" cried Donald.

"Hello," shouted Ronald.

"Hello!" Mr. Kilpatrick and Mr. McGillicuddy both called back.

"Oh, just wait till Halloween!" Donald shouted.

"Yes! Just wait," cried Ronald. "We're going to scare you."

"Me?" said Mr. Kilpatrick.

"Yes!" said Donald. "And Mr. McGillicuddy, too."

"You'll be awful scared," said Donald. And the twins rode off up the street while Mr. Kilpatrick drove away.

Every time the twins saw Mr. Kilpatrick or Mr. McGillicuddy they would say, "You're going to be scared. Just wait till Halloween."

The day before Halloween, Mr. Kilpatrick said to Mr. McGillicuddy, "You know, every Halloween the children around here get dressed up in their false faces and they have a great time, making me guess who they are. Some of them are certainly a sight. Enough to curdle your blood. I have to drive around and look 'em all over every year."

"What we ought to do this year," said Mr. McGillicuddy, "is to get dressed up ourselves and surprise them."

Mr. Kilpatrick laughed. "Mike, that would be a fine idea," he said, "but we have to stay in our uniforms. Can't drive a police car dressed up like witches or something."

"That's right!" said Mr. McGillicuddy. "But what's the matter with our getting some false faces? Exactly alike. We'll be twins."

"Mike, you're a wonder!" said Mr. Kilpatrick. "We'll do it. We'll do it. We'll surprise all the young ones in the neighborhood."

The two policemen drove to the store where Donald and Ronald had bought their false faces. They went inside. There was no one in the store but the shopkeeper. "Well, Mr. Kilpatrick," said the man, "it's a pleasure to see you. And Mr. McGillicuddy! What can I do for you?"

"We're looking for a couple of false faces," said Mr. Kilpatrick. "Something that will give all of those Halloweeners a real surprise."

The shopkeeper laughed. "Well, I think I can fix you up," he said. "How about one of these rubber ones? They're the best. They go right over your head." He laid one or two out on the counter.

Mr. Kilpatrick picked one up and put it on. It was a clown's face. Mr. Kilpatrick looked at himself in the mirror. "Sure, I can't go around in this," he said. "It would never do to have them say, 'Kilpatrick's a clown.'"

"How's this?" said Mr. McGillicuddy from inside another mask.

Mr. Kilpatrick looked at him. He was wearing the face of a monkey. "Oh, Mike!" cried Mr. Kilpatrick. "Don't make a monkey out of the police force."

Mr. Kilpatrick picked up another. He put it over his head.

"By cracky!" said Mr. McGillicuddy. "That's the worst face I've seen. 'Twould scare the liver right out of you on a dark night."

Mr. Kilpatrick looked at himself in the mirror. What he saw was a green face. It was the face of a troll. "Well, how about it, Mike?" he asked.

"It's all right with me," said Mr. McGillicuddy. "If you can stand looking at me, I can stand looking at you."

"Okay!" said Mr. Kilpatrick. "We'll take 'em."

The shopkeeper pulled out another mask exactly like the first one. He wrapped them both in a piece of paper and handed them to Mr. Kilpatrick.

The next day the twins could hardly wait to put on their faces and their Halloween costumes. Granny had dipped two pairs of pajamas into some green dye. Some parts were light green and some parts were dark green. When the boys were dressed, Granny said they certainly looked like real trolls.

"Are we ugly?" asked Donald.

"Well," said Granny, "you're certainly not pretty."

"We'll scare Mr. Kilpatrick," said Ronald.

About four o'clock the twin trolls went outside to wait for the red car to come by. "I hope Mr.

McGillicuddy's with Mr. Kilpatrick," said Donald.

"I do too," said Ronald.

The twins were too excited to ride their tricycles. They crawled behind the bushes on the front lawn, and every time anyone passed they jumped out and shouted, "Boo!"

About five o'clock they saw Mr. Kilpatrick's car turn the corner. They ran to the tree that grew by the curb. They hid behind the big trunk. The red car came along very slowly and stopped in front of the twins' house. The two little trolls heard Mr. Kilpatrick say, "Now where do you suppose those twins are?"

"Boo!" shouted the twins, jumping out.

Then they ran to the door of the car. They got there just as Mr. Kilpatrick stuck his head out of the window, and the two boys looked up into the green face and goggle eyes of a troll. Another troll was peering down at them over Mr. Kilpatrick's shoulder.

The two little trolls on the sidewalk screamed at the top of their lungs. Then they turned and ran as fast as they could, up the path to the house. At the front door they fell over each other, getting in.

"Granny! Granny!" they screamed.

"Trolls are in Mr. Kilpatrick's automobile. Trolls, Granny," cried Donald, "dressed up like policemen."

"Oh, no!" said Granny. "It can't be."

"Come see, Granny," said Ronald.

Granny went out in front. The little trolls kept behind Granny. Mr. Kilpatrick and Mr. McGillicuddy stepped out of the car. When Granny saw them, she began to laugh. She laughed and laughed. "Why, it's just Mr. Kilpatrick and Mr. McGillicuddy," she said to the twins. "You're not afraid of Mr. Kilpatrick and Mr. McGillicuddy."

"Come along," said Mr. Kilpatrick to the two

boys. "Let's walk down the street and see our other friends."

"Yes, let's!" said Ronald, putting one hand into Mr. McGillicuddy's and one into Mr. Kilpatrick's.

"We'll scare them, won't we?" said Donald, taking hold of Mr. Kilpatrick's other hand. So down the street went two policeman trolls and two little boy trolls.

"We scared you good, Mr. Kilpatrick," said Ronald.

"Yes! You were awful scared, weren't you, Mr. McGillicuddy?" said Donald.

"How about it, Mike?" said Mr. Kilpatrick. "Were you scared?"

"By cracky," said Mr. McGillicuddy, "I thought sure we would scare the twins."

"But you didn't," said Donald with a laugh. "I wasn't a bit scared."

"Neither was I," said Ronald. "I wasn't scared a bit."

Chapter 9

PENNIES FOR UNICEF

EDDIE WILSON was a collector. His family called most everything that he collected junk, but to Eddie it was all valuable property. One of his collections, however, was not considered junk by his family or by anyone else. It was his coin collection.

Eddie had decided to start the collection the

first time he heard his father use the word *numismatist.* Eddie's ears had perked up immediately, and he asked him what the word meant. When his father told him that a numismatist was a collector of coins, Eddie decided to be one. He was always fond of big words.

The very next day Eddie told his friend Boodles that he was a numismatist.

Boodles looked at Eddie in amazement. "You are?" Boodles exclaimed. "Gee, Eddie, I always thought you were an American."

Eddie laughed. "Of course I'm an American," he said. "A numismatist is a coin collector."

"Why don't you just say coin collector then?" Boodles asked.

"'Cause numismatist sounds more important," Eddie replied.

Eddie the numismatist began to learn which coins were the most valuable, and soon he knew a great deal about them. He liked all coins, but his greatest interest was in pennies. They came to him more easily than dimes or nickels, and some were very rare. Eddie was always examining pennies, hoping to find a valuable one.

One day near the end of September, when Eddie was reading the comic strip in the local paper, his eyes fell to the bottom of the page. There he saw the words, *Halloween Boy or Girl of the Year*. The announcement said that the boy or girl in his town who collected the most pennies for UNICEF on Halloween would be named Halloween Boy or Girl of the Year. In recognition, the child would be treated to a day in New York at the U.N., accompanied by a newspaper reporter and a photographer. Eddie decided then and there that he wanted to be Halloween Boy of the Year. His photograph might appear in newspapers all over the country.

Eddie dropped the paper and thought of all the pennies he would collect. Perhaps he would even get a valuable one, which would add to the amount that he turned in. Just another dollar or two might be all he needed to make him Halloween Boy of the Year.

Then Eddie realized with disappointment that he would have no chance to use his expertise. The UNICEF box the children carried when they went trick-or-treating was made so that they couldn't open it. People always put their pennies right into it, so how would he know if he had a valuable penny? Oh, well, Eddie thought. He could still become Halloween Boy of the Year by collecting the most pennies. Eddie began to look forward to Halloween more eagerly than ever before.

Halloween came on a Friday, and that morning Eddie's teacher, Mrs. Goodbee, handed out UNICEF boxes to all the children in his class. She told the children that the pennies collected for UNICEF went to help needy children all over the world, and she hoped they would bring in many pennies.

On Halloween night, Eddie was very excited. He went out early with his UNICEF box and a trick-or-treat bag. Like the early bird that caught the worm, he would catch the pennies.

Eddie knew all of the neighbors, and he called on them every Halloween. Now, dressed in an Indian suit and beautiful headdress, he went first to the house next door, where Mrs. Brooks and her sister, Miss Taylor, lived.

When Mrs. Brooks opened the door, she called out, "Come Sister, here's an Indian come to call. I hope he isn't on the warpath."

Miss Taylor came and looked at Eddie. "Oh, don't be afraid, Sister. I think he looks like a friendly Indian. In fact, I'll bet this Indian is Eddie Wilson."

Eddie took off his mask, and the two sisters laughed. Then Mrs. Brooks dropped some ginger cookies and a chocolate-covered marshmallow into Eddie's bag.

Eddie thanked them and held out his box. "Do

you have any pennies for UNICEF?" he asked.

Mrs. Brooks and Miss Taylor both dropped some pennies into Eddie's box.

"Thanks a lot," Eddie said again. "I'm hoping to be named Halloween Boy of the Year."

"Well, good luck to you!" said the two sisters, as they closed the door after Eddie.

As Eddie went from house to house he ate chocolates and candy and cookies and handfuls of sticky raisins. At each house he held out his UNICEF box and collected more pennies. Although Eddie kept licking his fingers, the UNICEF box began to get very sticky. Smears of chocolate and bits of marshmallow soon covered it completely.

When Eddie reached home, his parents were sitting in the living room. He called out that he was home and carried his box immediately to the desk in the family room. Poochie, Eddie's latest stray dog, came along right behind him. Smelling the cookies and candy, Poochie nuzzled Eddie's leg. Eddie gave him a piece of cookie, but when Poochie put his front paws on the edge of the desk and licked the UNICEF box, Eddie said, "Beat it, Poochie!"

Eddie moved the box, which now smelled like a bakery shop and a candy store rolled into one, farther back on the desk. But Poochie licked his chops and didn't move, hoping for another hand-out. "Scram, Poochie!" said Eddie. Disappointed, Poochie left the room with his tail between his legs.

Eddie sat at the desk and shook the UNICEF box several times. He had collected quite a few pennies, but he couldn't tell how many. As a numismatist, he longed to look at the pennies and see if there was a valuable one among them. But the UNICEF box could not be opened. It had to be taken to school, and only then could the pennies be taken out and counted. Never had Monday morning seemed such a long way off.

Eddie picked up the box again, and this time

he noticed the chocolate smears all over it. He guessed he ought to clean it up but decided to wait till morning. It was getting late, and he was beginning to feel sleepy.

Eddie went off to bed and fell asleep wondering whether he had enough pennies to make him Halloween Boy of the Year. When he woke up, he was still thinking about his pennies. Eddie dawdled as he dressed. There was no reason to hurry. The weekend ahead seemed endless.

Eddie was pulling on his sweater when he heard his mother calling. "Eddie, your breakfast is on the table."

"Okay!" Eddie called back. "I'm coming."

Eddie went downstairs and into the kitchen. His mother gave him a kiss on the top of his head and said, "How was Halloween?"

"Great!" said Eddie. "I got a lot of candy and a lot of pennies for my UNICEF box. Oh, Mom! I hope I have enough to be Halloween Boy of the Year."

"I hope so too!" said his mother.

Eddie sat down at the table. "Where is every-body?" he asked.

"The twins have gone to play football," said his mother, "and Rudy has gone to hockey practice. Dad is playing golf, and I'm going off to the market as soon as you finish your breakfast."

"Gee, I'll be all alone!" said Eddie. "I don't know what I'll do this morning. Boodles won't be coming over till later."

"Well, if I know my Eddie," said his mother, "you'll find something to do."

"I guess so!" said Eddie, laughing. "I just wish I knew how many pennies were in that UNICEF box. I just wish I knew."

Eddie finished his oatmeal and went to the sink, where he picked up a wet cloth. "I have to clean up my UNICEF box," he said to his mother. "I got some chocolate on it."

"All right, Eddie," said his mother. "I'll see you in a little while."

"'Bye, Mom," said Eddie, going off to the family room.

At the door Eddie stopped in his tracks. The wet cloth in his hand dropped to the floor. He couldn't believe his eyes. Bits of orange, white, and black cardboard lay all over the floor. His UNICEF box was torn into pieces, and the pennies inside of it were scattered all over the carpet.

"Eeks!" Eddie cried out. "What a mess! Poochie, how could you!" He knew his dog, with his fondness for sweets, was responsible for the havoc in the room.

Then Eddie thought of his teacher, Mrs. Goodbee. "She'll be hoppin' mad!" he said to himself. "She'll be furious. Oh, jeepers!"

Eddie stood looking down at the pennies, and suddenly he realized his wish had come true. Now he had a chance to count his pennies and check to see if there was a valuable one among them.

Quickly Eddie ran to the desk, where he found

a magnifying glass and an old candy box. Then he dropped on his knees and began to pick up the pennies. Eddie decided that this morning was going to be better than he had expected.

When Poochie came into the room, Eddie didn't know whether to scold him or pat him on the head. Instead, he just said, "Oh, Poochie, look what you did!" Poochie hung his head and licked one of the scraps of the UNICEF box.

Eddie was examining each penny under his magnifying glass when Boodles came in. As soon as he saw Eddie on the floor, Boodles cried out, "Eddie, what goes! Whatcha doin' on the floor?"

Eddie dropped a penny into the candy box and said, "Poochie tore up my UNICEF box, and I'm gathering up the pennies. Of course I'm looking at each one to see if it's valuable."

"Any luck?" Boodles asked.

"Not yet," Eddie replied, "but they're all over the floor." Eddie peered under the couch. "It's so dark under this couch that I can't see anything."

"I'll help you move it," said Boodles.

"Thanks!" said Eddie.

Together the two boys moved the couch, and Eddie picked up more pennies. As he dropped each one into the candy box, Eddie said, "No luck!"

"How many pennies have you got?" said Boodles.

"Two hundred and six so far," Eddie replied.

"That's just two dollars and six cents," said Boodles.

"That's right," said Eddie, sounding a bit depressed. "It isn't very much."

Then he said to Boodles, "Come, help me move this chair. There may be more pennies under it." Boodles helped Eddie move the chair, and Eddie picked up a few more pennies.

After most of the furniture in the family room had been moved, Eddie decided that he had gathered up all the pennies. There were now three hundred and sixty-seven in the candy box.

Unfortunately, Eddie had not found any that were worth more than one cent. He was disappointed. He didn't think three dollars and sixty-seven cents would make him Halloween Boy of the Year.

Just then Eddie's mother came in. "Hello, boys," she said, looking around the room. "Who moved all the furniture?"

"Oh, Boodles and I moved it," said Eddie. "I'm sorry, Mom, but Poochie tore up my UNICEF box and scattered the pennies all over the room. I picked them up, and I only collected three dollars and sixty-seven cents. I guess that won't make me Halloween Boy of the Year."

His mother patted him on the back and said, "Cheer up! It isn't the end of the world. Here, you two, let's put the furniture back."

They replaced the couch, the chair, and the other things that Eddie and Boodles had moved. On her way back to the kitchen, Mrs. Wilson called from the hall, "Here's a penny on the floor, Eddie. I guess it rolled out of the room."

Eddie jumped up and ran to his mother, holding out his hand. "Oh, let's see! Let's see!" he said. His mother gave Eddie the penny, and he ran back to get the magnifying glass.

Holding the glass over the penny, Eddie looked through it carefully. Suddenly he let out a yell. "Oh, Mom! It's a 1909 penny!" Eddie jumped up. "This is a valuable penny. Whoopee! I've found a valuable penny!"

"No kidding!" exclaimed Boodles. "How much is it worth? Maybe fifty cents or a dollar?"

"Maybe," Eddie replied. "I'm going to take it over to Mr. Reed at the coin shop and find out."

"Wouldn't it be great if it was worth a dollar!" said Boodles.

"Sure would!" Eddie answered. "Then I'd have four dollars and sixty-eight cents. Do you want to come with me? We can go over on our bikes."

"Sure!" said Boodles.

It didn't take the boys long to pedal over to the

coin shop on Main Street. Quickly they parked their bicycles and rushed inside.

When Mr. Reed saw Eddie, he said, "Hello, Sonny! What can I do for you this morning?"

"I've got a penny here," said Eddie, "and I think it's a valuable one."

"Sounds good," said Mr. Reed. "Put it right here on the counter, and I'll look at it under the magnifying glass."

Eddie put his hand in his pocket and felt for the penny. It wasn't there. "Gee," said Eddie, "I put it in my pocket, but I can't find it."

"Maybe you put it in your shirt pocket," suggested Mr. Reed.

Eddie felt in his shirt pocket. "I know I put it in my pants pocket," said Eddie, pushing his hand down into his pocket again.

"Well, pull your pockets inside out," said Boodles.

Eddie pulled his pockets inside out, but there was no penny.

"Look, Eddie," said Boodles, "jump up and down. Maybe it'll fall out."

Eddie jumped up and down, but nothing dropped on the floor.

"Maybe if you turn a somersault, it'll come out," said Boodles.

Eddie turned a somersault. No penny appeared.

"Well, say, Eddie," said Boodles. "Maybe you swallowed it."

"Swallowed it!" Eddie cried.

Just then Mr. Reed's mother came in from the room in the back of the shop. "Now, Sonny," she said, "if you've swallowed a penny, you'll need a dose of milk of magnesia right away."

"I didn't swallow the penny," said Eddie. "I don't put pennies in my mouth."

"Well, then, you don't have to take a dose of milk of magnesia," said Mr. Reed's mother.

Eddie looked relieved. "I know I put that penny into my right-hand pocket. I know I did."

Mr. Reed leaned over and said to Eddie, "Maybe you've got a hole in your pocket. Look and see."

Eddie felt in his pocket once more. Then he cried, "You're right! I've got a hole in my pocket."

"I sure hope that penny didn't drop out of your pants on the way here," said Mr. Reed.

"Let's look around our bikes," Boodles said. "It may have dropped out when you got off your bike."

"Boy, I hope we find it!" said Eddie, as he opened the door.

Boodles and Mr. Reed followed Eddie to where the bicycles were standing. They looked all around on the sidewalk. "Don't see it," said Boodles.

Just then Eddie cried out, "I've found it! I've found it!" There, in the gutter of the street, half hidden by some leaves, was the missing penny.

Eddie picked it up, and they all went back into the shop. Anxiously Eddie handed the penny to Mr. Reed, who put it under his magnifying glass. Eddie held his breath.

Mr. Reed let out a low whistle. Then he looked at Eddie and said, "Sonny, you're in luck. It's a beauty! This 1909 Lincoln penny is worth five hundred dollars today."

"Five hundred dollars!" Boodles cried out. "Oh, Eddie!"

Eddie was speechless. He just stood with his mouth open, staring at the penny. Then he looked at Mr. Reed and said, "Honest?"

Mr. Reed laughed. "That's right," he said, giving the penny back to Eddie.

Carefully Eddie examined his left-hand pocket. When he was sure that it did not have a hole, he put the penny in it. "Thanks, Mr. Reed, for the good news," he said. "Now I want to get this penny home before I lose it again."

On the way back to Eddie's house, Boodles called out, "Say, Eddie! Are you going to keep that penny?"

Eddie was quiet for a moment. Then he said, "Well, I never thought I'd find such a valuable penny. Of course, it would be great to keep it. But I can't, Bood. I collected that penny for UNICEF, so it belongs to UNICEF." Eddie brightened. "Now I'll be giving five hundred and three dollars and sixty-eight cents to UNICEF."

"Oh, Eddie!" exclaimed Boodles. "You'll be sure to be Halloween Boy of the Year. I don't think anybody will beat that."

When Eddie told his family about the five-hundred-dollar penny, everyone was excited. "Gee, Eddie," said his brother Rudy. "UNICEF ought to be awfully glad that you were smart enough to find that penny."

Then his brother Joe spoke up. "Too bad you can't keep it, Eddie."

The other twin, Frank, answered, "Well, he can't, 'cause it belongs to UNICEF."

The discussion was beginning to make Eddie feel wistful, but he cheered up when he remembered how much he wanted to be Halloween Boy of the Year. There would be other chances to add valuable pennies to his collection, he was sure. Certainly he would continue looking for them.

On Monday, Eddie took all the pennies to school in the old candy box. He kept the 1909 penny separate, however, and carried it in an envelope. When he gave the box and the envelope to Mrs. Goodbee, he explained what had happened and that the 1909 penny was worth five hundred dollars.

"Why, Eddie! How wonderful!" she exclaimed.

When the children in the class heard the news, they gasped in surprise. All of them watched intently as Mrs. Goodbee put the 1909 penny into a little box just as though it were a precious jewel, and Eddie felt very proud. "I'll take this penny to Mr. Reed," she said. "He'll tell me the best way to get it to UNICEF, and I'll be sure you get proper credit, Eddie."

Clearly Eddie would be named Halloween Boy of the Year.

A week or so later Eddie received a letter from the newspaper telling him that he was the winner of the Halloween contest. Then he received another one from UNICEF. It said:

Dear Eddie Wilson:

We have received your penny worth $500, and we congratulate you for recognizing its value. Your generosity in contributing it to the UNICEF drive is much appreciated. You are not only a numismatist but a philanthropist.

We look forward to greeting you when you

visit the U.N., where you will be photographed with the Secretary-General.

Sincerely,
UNICEF

When he finished reading the letter, Eddie said to his father, "Just think, Dad. I'm going to be photographed with the Secretary-General of the U.N.! I guess that makes me a very famous person."

Mr. Wilson looked at Eddie and said, "Yes, Eddie, it does! But don't let it go to your head. You're not president of the United States yet."

Eddie read the letter again. Then he said, "Dad, what's a philanthropist?"

"A philanthropist," said his father, "is someone who is generous and gives his money away."

"Oh," said Eddie. "That's right. That's me!" He was pleased. He had discovered another big word to add to his collection.

ABOUT THE AUTHOR

Carolyn Haywood was born in Philadelphia and now lives in Chestnut Hill, a suburb of that city. A graduate of the Philadelphia Normal School, she also studied at the Pennsylvania Academy of Fine Arts, where she won the Cresson European Scholarship. Her first story, "B" IS FOR BETSY, was published in 1939. Since then she has written books almost every year and has become one of the most widely read American writers for younger children.